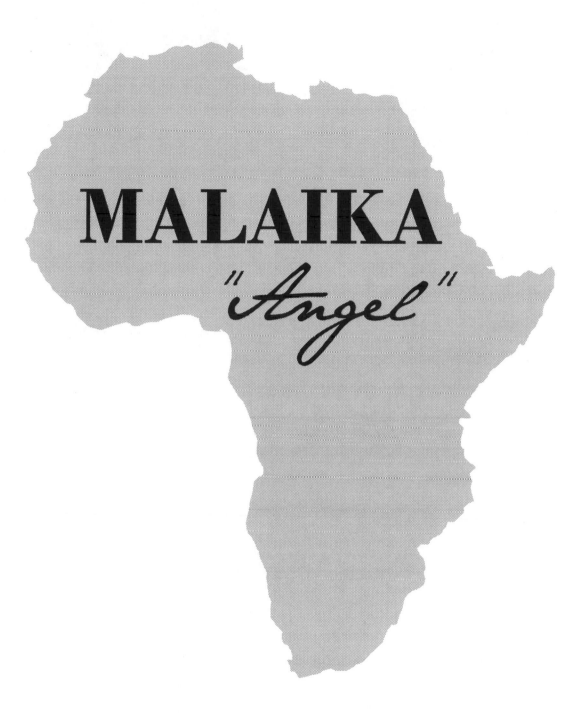

MALAIKA
"Angel"

Kwabena Date-Bah, MBA, LLM, LLB

authorHOUSE®

AuthorHouse™ UK Ltd.
500 Avebury Boulevard
Central Milton Keynes, MK9 2BE
www.authorhouse.co.uk
Phone: 08001974150

Published by AuthorHouse 3/15/2013

ISBN: 978-1-4817-8792-5 (sc)
ISBN: 978-1-4817-8793-2 (e)

Any people depicted in stock imagery provided by Thinkstock are models,
and such images are being used for illustrative purposes only.
Certain stock imagery © Thinkstock.

This book is printed on acid-free paper.

Because of the dynamic nature of the Internet, any web addresses or links contained in this
book may have changed since publication and may no longer be valid.

The views expressed in this work are solely those of the author and do not necessarily reflect the
views of the publisher, and the publisher hereby disclaims any responsibility for them.

I would like to dedicate "Malaika" to my wife, Mrs. Victoria Date-Bah, for her continuous encouragement and support.

Table of Contents

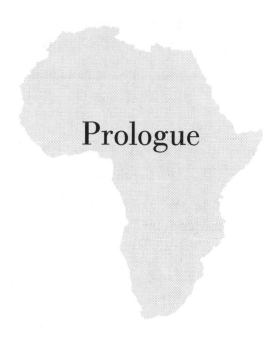

Prologue

"Greg, Greg, where are you? Come and remove your dirty boots from the hallway!"

Greg Agyemang – a black African sixth-former already six-foot-one – could hear Aunt Ethel calling to him from the lobby downstairs in their small end-of-terrace home in Northwood, North London. His mud-stained size-nine football boots lay dripping wet on the cream carpet of the lobby downstairs. Dark-skinned Auntie Ethel, still pretty though advancing in age, was his only living relative since his father, a wealthy Gold Coast trader, and his Kenyan mother, a housewife, had died in a horrific road accident in June 1949 in the country of his birth, the Gold Coast.

Despite his impending STEP exams for possible entrance to Cambridge University and his lack of preparation and review for those life-changing exams, Greg found it impossible to tear himself away from his football passion and his dream that one day he might be good enough to play for Chelsea Football Club. He lay on his bed, listening to a West Indian calypso band, the Shadows, and Elvis Presley on his small bedside radio. This music was very popular with the students at the boys' school that Greg now attended in England – Merchant Taylors Public School in Northwood, Middlesex.

As far as Ethel was concerned, Greg was *malaika* because his presence in her home had rescued her from her previous frequent bouts of depression and unbearable solitude. Her solitude had become unbearable since the untimely death of the love of her life some fifteen years before, the white English coffee trader she had married. He had brought her to the UK only some five years before his death. This loneliness

5

was compounded by the fact that Ethel had been unable to give her husband a child, so she was her husband's only heir. The several doctors that they had consulted said that she was barren, and they had no fertility treatment that would help. Despite this loneliness, she loved her anglicised lifestyle in England and was in no rush to go back to her relatives in Kenya, even though she could live in a position of some opulence and esteem in Nairobi. The occasional incidents of racist abuse and violence she faced in London did not deter her, even though she had also suffered terribly during the smog in London in 1952. She loved her role as Greg's Paraclete.

As Greg trudged home from Merchant Taylors Public School football practice one cold winter evening in December 1955 with his school friends, his mind switched to the huge amounts of review he needed to do if he was to be successful in his Cambridge exams. He had only arrived in England three years before when he disembarked from the liner ship at Southampton Harbour. When he arrived at the port, he saw a large number of other black people and Asian people disembarking from another large ship moored to the port. Auntie Ethel, who had come to meet him and take him home, told him that these people had travelled to the UK from the West Indies as part of the Wind-Rush to take up the promises of work that the British government had made to them. Greg had never even heard of the West Indies before then.

Since his parents' premature death, Greg had been cared for by his father's working-class farmer friend, Uncle Kwaku, in the Akropong Hills, along with Uncle Kwaku's large family, including his six children. When his parents died, Greg had been exposed to real financial and emotional hardship because his more affluent relatives had disowned him and taken the financial inheritance that his parents had left for him. However, his mother's only sibling – her sister living in London, England – upon hearing about his plight, had sent for him.

Auntie Ethel had been able to pay for Greg's expensive education through the money she had inherited from her late husband. Even though he was the only black person in his class in England, he felt he belonged because his classmates made him feel welcome. They always wanted him to recount his experiences in the hot tropics of Africa. This was in stark contrast to the way the white Europeans treated him when he was out in the town. He enjoyed telling these stories.

Greg now sat at his desk in his reasonably proportioned bedroom with tension slowly creeping from his shoulders to his head as he delved into his history notes in a brave attempt to review for those Cambridge entrance exams he would be facing in a week's time.

His aunt reluctantly removed his football boots herself and put them in the sink in the utility room. Then she started to clean them. He had been her primary source of pride and comfort since the premature death of her husband from lung cancer. She could not bear the thought that one day soon he might be leaving home to go to university. However, she had accepted it as a necessary evil if he was to achieve the dreams and goals she had in mind for him.

As Greg recapped his notes on the triumphs of King George VI and the achievements of the relatively new native colonial administration in the Gold Coast with Dr Kwame Nkrumah as its prime minister, his nostrils twitched at the wondrous smells wafting into his room from the kitchen downstairs. It seemed that Auntie Ethel had cooked another chicken casserole masterpiece with fried noodles. The prospect of savouring this delicious food was too tempting! Within five minutes, he had rushed downstairs and dished himself a large helping of the sumptuous food.

Auntie Ethel said, "Greg, wash your hands before you tuck into your meal. Also don't forget to say grace."

"Yes, Auntie," he said with a sheepish smile on his face.

She then returned to the utility room to finish cleaning Greg's boots. She could hear Greg talking in careless whispers on the telephone. Auntie Ethel was very proud that Greg was basically a morally upright boy, despite the many upheavals he had had in his life. However, he seemed to have inherited his father's preference for pursuing several sexual dalliances at the same time. He never seemed satisfied. Nor did he seem to appreciate how he hurt the many girls he left broken-hearted in his wake. Those white English girls saw Greg as a kind of exotic fruit to be savoured. He was going to land her and himself both in trouble one day soon.

She called to him, "You had better hit those books again. You will not get your Cambridge blue for football if you do not study." She dreamt that he would study law at Cambridge and then become a barrister – a Queen's Counsel! Whoa, that would be something.

As she walked into the lounge, she had a look through the windows. It had been a very cold winter's day, the sort of day when she was glad that she had stayed mainly at home. Some lonely souls huddled past her windows on their way to their homes. The street lights were coming on. and the yellowish hue gave the front of their home a kind of magical quality. She loved her home, even though her neighbours were not especially friendly towards her despite her repeated efforts to engage them in conversation. She drew comfort and strength from her attendance at a Presbyterian church with a largely African congregation in Willesden. There, she had also been able to introduce Greg to some African boys and girls to help him to feel more settled in London and also to help him to remember his African identity. There were a few Ghanaians there so that Greg was able to practise the Twi language he had spoken as a very young boy. At home, Auntie Ethel taught him a little Swahili.

After she had drawn the curtains, she switched on the radio, which was tuned to the BBC World Service. She settled into her favourite green armchair and listened to the current affairs programme. She heard an interesting speech given by Prime Minister Anthony Eden at the House of Commons.

She had had a very tiring day, particularly chasing after Greg, and at her stage of life, she was glad of the rest when it came. Soon she was lightly snoring as she dozed. An unconscious smile crossed her face as she dreamt of her many pleasant walks with her late husband. She remembered fondly the many times they had run along the sandy beaches in Mombasa, Kenya, hand in hand, ecstatic in each other's company and without a care in the world. She really missed him!

In the meantime, Greg had been deeply engrossed in his reading and general review when he heard his aunt's snoring from downstairs. He thought this would be an opportune moment for him to sneak out of the house to go and see his sweetheart of the moment, pretty Sally Smith with the strawberry-blond hair, who attended nearby St Helen's School in Northwood, Middlesex. He knew that he was taking a risk, but he did not care. Long ago Greg had decided that life was to be enjoyed and he was simply adhering to his philosophy. As he crept out of the house, he felt guilty about the panic he would cause Auntie Ethel when she woke up and found that he was gone. However, he decided that he would not stay out long. He could not see far ahead of him because of the dense fog which had descended over the High Street in Northwood. The street lamps gave scant illumination.

Suddenly, Greg saw a pretty girl with a familiar mane of strawberry-blond hair in front of him. When she heard his footsteps, she turned around, and Greg found himself in front of his current sweetheart. Sally was out walking the family dog, Trickster, with her elder brother, Winston. Her brother did not really approve of Greg, but he knew how happy Greg made his sister and was not going to get in the way of her happiness.

Also, Sally's brother was also partial to a bit of jungle fever; much to the chagrin of his parents, he was dating a Nigerian princess who was attending St Helen's.

Sally spread her warm arms all around Greg and they lingered in a warm embrace for a few moments. Then, with little thought as to whether Winston was still watching, they engaged in a French kiss, which was so delicious that Greg could feel that he was getting stiff in his loins. His pulse began to race. He began to fondle her large breasts whilst he licked the flavour of her tongue in his mouth. He wondered what it would be like to make love to the beautiful Sally. What a mouth-watering prospect! Suddenly, he saw the frown on Winston's face. Greg knew it was time to bid his farewell to Sally and return home to his aunt, who he hoped would still be asleep in her armchair, blissfully unaware of his dalliances tonight.

Sally said, "See you after school tomorrow."

"I am really looking forward to it. Thank you, Winston, and good-bye, both of you."

Greg turned around and raced back down the High Street to his home. He fumbled through his pockets for his house keys, quickly opened the front door, and entered the lobby.

As he started climbing the stairs, Auntie Ethel stirred. "Is that you, Greg?"

" I just came downstairs to take a break from my review."

"Get to bed; otherwise you will not be able to get up early to go to school tomorrow."

Greg said, "Good night, then."

"Good night, my love."

—m—

The next morning, Greg was awakened at 8.15 by Auntie Ethel, rudely interrupting his sweet dreams about Sally. He would be late to school if he did not rush. He did not even clean his teeth or wash his face. He simply threw his clothes on and grabbed his schoolbag and a slice of toast on his way to the front door. Then he ran to join his schoolmates, who were already a long way down the High Street.

The Cambridge STEP exams were only a few days away. However, he did not care about them at the moment because Sally had stolen his heart in a way unlike any other girl before her. He was daydreaming of setting up home with her and having kids, which was quite unlike him.

Suddenly, Greg bumped his head into a lamp post. The shock of the collision knocked him to the ground. His school friends who had been watching him from afar, started to laugh at him. After rubbing his forehead gingerly, Greg ran up to them and continued with them to school.

His best friend, Brian Dunton, a Geordie, was telling them that he believed that this season would be Newcastle United's turn to triumph in the Football First Division. Brian was singing the praises of the esteemed Newcastle striker, Jackie Milburn. He had already won the FA Cup with Newcastle United, three times and Brian was confident that Jackie could transfer his cup form to the Football First Division.

Brian asked Greg, "Are you going to football practice after school?"

"Yes, but I may be a little late."

Brian laughed. "I guess that means that you will be doing extracurricular activities with Sally again!" Brian himself was dating a Geordie girl, Rose Thompson, who attended St Margaret's School in Bushey. However, his romance did not seem to have the passion and intensity that Greg had recently experienced in his love life.

Greg smiled broadly. He felt very happy. First, though, he had to overcome the hurdles of the day's school lessons, starting with double Latin.

In the meantime, Sally was arriving at St Helen's School. She was similarly up in the clouds about her current beau, Greg. She had always had a predilection for darker-skinned boys and young men. However, until she met Greg, the closest she had come to her romantic fantasies were pictures of these epeople in magazines and books. She was overjoyed that Greg had come along. Even though he had a reputation for being a bit of a lady's man, she hoped she could tame him by holding out the promise of fulfilling all his sexual and romantic fantasies.

This posed a challenge, because, due to her strong Catholic faith, she felt honour-bound not to have sexual intercourse with Greg until they were married, unlike the other schoolgirls. She knew she would have her work cut out! Still, she hoped that she could rely on her elder brother, Winston, to persuade Greg to behave decently towards her. Oh the joys of young love!

Sally knew that Greg was one of the most intelligent boys in his class. Equally, she knew that he was obsessed with playing football and had an aptitude for the game, being a natural athlete and unusually tall. She and Auntie Ethel had encouraged

Greg to take the STEP Cambridge entrance examinations to read law at Cambridge University, even though Greg made it clear that his football dream was his real passion. He still had aspirations to be a professional footballer and to play against Sir Stanley Matthews in an important match like the FA Cup Final, where he would show the great maestro some dribbling turns of his own. He had watched TV clips of Matthews playing in the FA Cup Final of 1953, where he displayed such wing wizardry that every football supporter was in awe of him. Greg wanted to play just like him. However, whenever Greg told Sally about this goal of his, she claimed that he was tilting at the windmills. This only inspired him to take his football practice and school matches more seriously.

Occasionally, the front door of the house that Auntie Ethel and Greg shared in Northwood was sprayed with the large letters *KBW*, standing for "Keep Britain White." This always frightened them. However, Sally's parents organised support within the local community for Greg and Ethel. This support dissipated when the 1958 Notting Hill race riots occurred. Despite these racial tensions, Auntie Ethel always reminded Greg to be as friendly and as polite as possible.

Greg's Birth and Childhood
in the Gold Coast

Greg was the only child of a tall, sanguine African native trader in the Gold Coast, Mr Derek Akwasi Agyemang, who hailed from the bustling town of Kumasi in the Ashanti region, deep in the hinterland of the Gold Coast. His mother, Ruth, was a tall, beautiful and tall black African lady, who came from a poor Kikuyu family based in Nairobi in Kenya. They had met when Greg's father came to Kenya on one of his many business trips.

Derek. Agyemang was a prosperous cocoa and coffee trader, who had taken over his own father's Ghanaian export firm. Thanks to the success of Greg's grandfather in conducting his cocoa business, Derek had led a privileged existence, including a good education at Mfantsipim School. He had run school trading projects with his classmates, which had helped him to develop his commercial expertise. Moreover, he had a natural business acumen, which helped him expand the cocoa business profitably and quickly. His business grew from strength to strength, and he was able to rent plush new offices in the centre of Kumasi and in Accra, another town in the Gold Coast, where he received many clients. A wide variety of women also flocked to Derek Agyemang, so that he maintained several sexual and romantic relationships with them at the same time.

As time went on, his business took him further afield. He was eventually travelling to other African countries, such as Côte d'Ivoire and Kenya. He dreamed of travelling to the UK and the USA, but no business opportunities had yet appeared that would require him to travel in those directions. Greg's paternal grandfather, Kwaku Agyemang, told his son of his journeys to America and England. He told him that despite his joy at seeing these foreign lands and their lifestyles and customs, which were different from what he experienced in the Gold Coast, he suffered from terrible racial discrimination. He found this especially hard to take because he was accustomed to receiving preferential treatment wherever he went in the Gold Coast. His tales of those bad experiences did not dampen Derek's enthusiasm to travel to the USA and to the UK.

Because his business expanded significantly after he inherited it from his father, Derek Akwasi Agyemang wanted to explore any possible market in the UK and the USA for his cocoa and coffee produce. On a visit to Kenya by ship in 1935, he met a beautiful tall Kikuyu lady in a grocers' shop in the commercial district of Nairobi. The lady was serving at the counter. Derek was attracted by her beautiful smile and infectious laugh. He loved the plaits in her hair. She could only manage a few words in English and often resorted to her native Swahili, much to Derek's consternation, who did not understand a word of that language. Nevertheless, he was entranced by the innate beauty of the Kikuyu lady, the future Mrs Ruth Agyemang. Within a few short weeks, they had returned to Kumasi, where they had a grand wedding. There they settled until the birth of Greg in 1938.

Shortly after Greg's birth, the young Agyemang family moved to live in Accra. Derek's business was thriving, and he needed to be in closer contact with his important clients in the colony's capital city. Despite the family's frequent visits to Kumasi to visit Derek's parents – they died of old age within a few months of each other in 1942 – the young Agyemang family tried to consolidate their new social and business networks in Accra.

Greg and his parents moved to a three-bedroom detached house in the cantonments area of Accra. There he enjoyed playing football with the other children from his neighbourhood in the local park. From a young age, his father enrolled him at Achimota School, and he started attending that school in addition to home tuition because his father had big ambitions for him. This meant that Greg's level of reading, writing, and arithmetic were quite advanced for his age. All the while his parents were trying to have another child, but without any success.

One evening in June 1949 attended Derek and Ruth Agyemang a CPP Party Rally at the Accra Polo Grounds at which the great Kwame Nkrumah spoke. Because Derek and Ruth knew that they would be home late, they had left Greg with their Fante neighbours, Auntie Ekua and Uncle Kwesi and their son, Kobina, for the night. It had been raining most of the day, but it had stopped raining in the late afternoon, so Derek and Ruth felt that they could go to the rally in comfort and some safety. Derek wore his kente cloth with his khaki shorts, and Ruth wore a black and white European dress.

Having been moved by the great Mr Nkrumah and believing that their dream of "self-government now" for the Gold Coast Africans was at last within reach, they had drunk a toast to Mr Nkrumah and to Ghanaian independence. Derek drank a bit more than he should have, and his spatial senses were impaired. However, his bravado encouraged him to insist on driving. As they left their friends at the end of the rally to make for home in their Jaguar car, it began to rain quite heavily. Within ten minutes after they started their drive, the road became so muddy and slippery that the going was quite difficult.

Presently they had to drive up a steep hill. Despite his drunken stupor, Derek was alert enough to be quite concerned about the treacherous road conditions. Suddenly a large lorry, overloaded with timber, was approaching them from the opposite direction. It started to skid on the road and a head-on collision with Derek and Ruth's car was inevitable. There was an almighty crash, and blood and body parts gushed out of the vehicles.

Early the next morning, Greg was woken up by Auntie Ekua, who brought him a large cup of hot chocolate. Then she told him the tragic news of his parents' death in a car accident the night before. Greg could not believe her; at first, he thought it was a sick joke or prank that Kobina had asked his mother to play on him. However, when he saw the tears in Auntie Ekua's eyes, he realised that his nightmare was just beginning. He curled up into a ball and sobbed uncontrollably. He could not believe that his loving and humorous parents were no more, and he wondered what he was going to do to survive.

Soon he learned how cruel his relatives could be when it came to money and his financial future. They persuaded Greg's parents' lawyers to leave them in sole charge of Greg's money in a trust until he should reach adulthood. However, in the meantime, they passed Greg on to Kwaku, his father's working-class farmer friend in Akropong, under strict instructions not to tell Greg of the money that his parents had left him. In exchange for this secrecy, they would supply the farmer with regular payments, with which to look after Greg, amongst other things. The trustees started to spend Greg's money so that it was all frittered away long before he was anywhere near the age of adulthood.

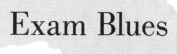

Exam Blues

Greg could not believe that the crucial Cambridge STEP Exams were upon him. He wished he had spent more time reviewing his notes instead of examining the delicate pink flesh of Sally's bosom. The latter had obviously given him more pleasure.

Auntie Ethel had warned him that hubris could get the better of him. His intelligence and arrogance would take a huge knock if he was unsuccessful in his attempt to secure a place at Cambridge University. He tried desperately to gather his thoughts as he waited to enter the exam room to do his general paper with the other special group of elite students from Merchant Taylors' School who had been entered for the Oxbridge exams. They were all familiar faces, but Greg was in no mood for conversation. He knew how disappointed Auntie Ethel would be if he did not manage to secure a place at Cambridge University and that he would be missing out on the trip to Paris she had promised him.

Suddenly, thoughts of Sally's flowing strawberry blond hair came into his mind. He was really looking forward to seeing her at the end of his exam. He found the prospect of this rendezvous relaxing. He continued to wonder how Sally had changed him from a serial womaniser to being a respectable settling-down type. His best friend, Brian, told him that a beautiful woman had the guile to make you do anything if she really put her mind to it.

The teacher, Mr Truman, recalled him to the moment by saying, "Will you please enter the exam room now?"

Greg was gripped with stage fright. Then he thought of his aspirations to be a Cambridge fresher – the many sunny and steamy afternoons spent punting on the river among the spires in Cambridge. He steadied himself and walked into the room.

He sat down at his designated desk, opened his pencil-case, and took out his favourite blue fountain pen. Then, after a short prayer, he quietly waited to be invited to open the paper and begin the exam.

When Mr Truman announced, "You may open the paper and begin your exam," Greg's palms were suddenly moist. However, he thought of the wondrous pleasure that Sally had given him over the last few months and the famous Cambridge alumni that he admired so much, and this helped him bring his nerves under control.

The exam paper was a lot more difficult than he had expected. Only a few of the topics he had reviewed appeared on the paper. An hour later, Greg was halfway through his general studies STEP exam. To his relief, he had been able to improvise, relying on his general knowledge and his much-vaunted writing style.

Half an hour into the exam, he had heard some loud sobbing. He wondered who it was. He gave a curt glance around the room and saw that it was his best friend, Brian. He seemed to be holding his exam paper with tears streaming down his face. At first, Greg thought that Brian was being faint-hearted. Later, Greg was to find out that none of the subjects that Brian had reviewed had come up, and he found it extremely difficult to improvise.

Brian was a candidate for a degree of Politics, Philosophy, and Economics (PPE) at St Hugh's College at Oxford University. He was following a family tradition started by his grandfather and continued by his father of attending St Hugh's and taking a degree of Politics, Philosophy, and Economics. Both his grandfather and his father had become MPs and pursued ministerial careers within the Conservative government. Brian was beside himself with disappointment, thinking that he had let down his family and its good name. However, Greg had the credulous belief that everything would turn out fine for Brian because his father would sort it out for him.

At the end of his general studies exam, Greg was exhausted. His concentration had wavered for the last hour of the exam, with Sally seldom far from his mind. He hoped he could see her this afternoon or early evening. He knew he would be busy reviewing for his Cambridge history exam.

As he trudged out of the exam room barely able to keep himself awake because of his sheer mental exhaustion, he heard a familiar, beloved voice: "Greg, darling, over here! How did your exam go?"

He looked over his shoulder to find the strawberry-blond-haired beauty he loved so much standing next to Auntie Ethel. His aunt was shivering, and he thought that it was because of the cold December wind. As they walked towards Auntie Ethel's home, all three of them holding hands, Auntie Ethel told him that her shivering resulted from her nervousness and excitement at Greg's attempt to get into Cambridge University. She desperately hoped that he would be successful. If he succeeded in his endeavour, he would be the first of her relatives, friends, or acquaintances who had achieved this feat. Three more days of these exams and anguish, and Greg would be free to enjoy the company and bodily pleasures that Sally provided him.

When they got home, Auntie Ethel prepared a hearty meal of bangers and mash, which all three of them enjoyed. Then they chatted enthusiastically as they discussed their plans for the upcoming Christmas celebrations. They laughed a lot at Greg's plans of where he would take Sally in Paris if he managed to gain admission to Cambridge University. He was very keen on seeing the Eiffel Tower, the Notre Dame Cathedral, the Louvre, and the Palais de Justice. He also wanted to go for a cruise on the River Seine.

Auntie Ethel told her young charges that she wanted to catch the news. So she got up from her chair and switched on the radio. The tune "Santa Baby," sung by Ms. Eartha Kitt, was blaring out of the radio. Auntie Ethel wiggled her hips. She had loved this song since she had first heard it in 1953 and she was glad she could enjoy it in the pleasant company of Greg and Sally. Then the newsreader came on and was talking about the racial civil rights disobedience occurring in Montgomery, Alabama, in December 1955, when all the blacks were boycotting the bus service.

Suddenly they heard a knock on the front door. Auntie Ethel went to open the door and found Winston, Sally's elder brother, standing there. "Hello, Ms. Ethel," he said. "I have come to collect Sally to take her home."

"Hello, Winston, come in. Would you like a cup of tea?"

"Yes, that would be lovely."

Auntie Ethel quickly prepared a cup of tea for Winston and brought him a slice of cake. After he had enjoyed the food and drink, he asked Sally if they could leave.

Sally looked at Greg wistfully and then kissed him passionately on the lips. Next, she embraced Auntie Ethel and kissed her on both cheeks. She then moved briskly towards the front door and left with her brother.

— ∿ —

Shortly after Sally had left, Greg rose from the dining table and collected all the dirty dishes. He took them through to the kitchen, set them in the sink, and proceeded to do the washing up. Auntie Ethel stood behind him and watched him with pride. A few months ago, this occurrence would have been inconceivable. She was astounded at how much of an impact Sally had had on him.

However, he looked sad. As she continued to stand there, Auntie Ethel looked at him with growing concern in her eyes. Finally she said, "Don't worry, you will see her tomorrow."

"I know. That's not what I am worried about. I do not know how I am going to survive these Cambridge exams. I am suddenly very aware of how much it means to you that I succeed."

"I know that you will not let me down."

Upon hearing those words, Greg left the kitchen and climbed the stairs to his room. He sat down at his desk and opened his file. He was aiming to review his history notes tonight for the history STEP exam the next day. However, within half an hour of reading about Winston Churchill and the Allied invasion of Normandy, his head had slumped over his notes, and he was snoring.

The sound of his snoring interrupted Auntie Ethel's listening to the BBC World Service. She rose from her favourite green armchair and slowly climbed the stairs to go to his bedroom. (The stairs now posed a real difficulty to her weak frame. However, Greg had persuaded her that it was useful exercise for her to continue to struggle up the stairs.) When she reached his bedroom door, she knocked lightly on it and waited a few moments for an answer. Not hearing his voice, she decided to enter his room and found him slumped over his desk. She gently woke him up and led him to his bed, where she proceeded to cover him with his blanket. As he settled into the white soft sheets of his bed, Auntie Ethel was overcome by an urge to protect her treasure, Greg. She decided to turn in herself, after going back downstairs to turn off the radio.

Half an hour later, she lay quietly in her bed upstairs, praying hard that God would grant her wish that Greg would be admitted to Cambridge University. After fifteen minutes of her godly supplications, she closed her eyes and drifted off to sleep.

The next day, Greg awoke at 6 a.m., refreshed. He even managed to do an hour's review before he changed into his school clothes, cleaned his teeth, and descended the stairs. He grabbed two slices of toast and a cup of tea. Then, after wishing his aunt a pleasant day, he rushed out of the front door. Today he had the history paper, and he was rather looking forward to it.

Greg and Sally's Spring
Break in Paris – April 1956

Starry-eyed, Greg and Sally boarded the ship at Dover, bound for Calais. By the dockside, Auntie Ethel and Sally's family frantically waved good-bye to the young couple. Despite their many misgivings, Greg and Sally were going to Paris for a long weekend because Greg had won a place at Cambridge University to read law.

The couple remained on the deck for a good half an hour, waving to their relatives and beaming with excitement at the prospect of exploring Paris for a whole weekend all on their own. When the port at Dover was out of sight, they decided to walk around the deck of the ship, taking in the scenery. However, the cold winds soon persuaded them to go inside to their cabin below.

After they had spent an hour conversing, kissing, and embracing, Sally ceded to temptation. However, much to Greg's disappointment, because of her views on her Catholic faith, she would not allow Greg to have true intercourse with her. She only offered to please him orally, which he gratefully accepted. Within a minute, Greg and Sally were moaning uncontrollably, their grunts very much in sync. A few seconds later, Greg experienced an orgasm, the like of which he was never again to experience. Even though he had had sex before, this ejaculation had given him more pleasure than he had ever had.

For minutes afterwards, he was moaning Sally's name. He was desperate to make love to her in the conventional sense. However, she was determined that this should not happen. So he reluctantly accepted the frequent oral sex Sally offered him over the weekend.

By midmorning the next day, Greg and Sally had arrived in Calais. They disembarked and took a taxi to the Calais train station. Once they were there, they caught a train for Paris. The train seemed to take forever to arrive. However, Greg and Sally enjoyed the wondrous views of the French countryside. They saw many chateaux, rivers, and vineyards.

That evening, the train pulled into the Gare du Nord station. When they got off the train, Greg and Sally headed towards the exit of the station. Sally spoke French fluently and was able to arrange a taxi for them with no trouble. French was something else that Greg would have to learn on this trip – the other being patience. Within forty-five minutes, they were at their hotel beside the Eiffel Tower.

Ever since they had left Dover, Greg had been attracting hostile snares from those around him, because he was one of the few black men around, and he had a beautiful white woman on his arm. However, a part of him put it down to envy.

After a dinner of lamb cutlets and roast potatoes, they retired for the night. Even though they shared the same bed, they did not sleep together because Greg decided to be a gentleman and to respect Sally's wishes.

The next day after a hearty breakfast of croissants, black coffee and ham, they caught a bus to the Champs-Élysées. There they explored the different boutiques. Then they climbed up the road to see the Arc de Triomphe. It gave them a wonderful view of the different parts of Paris.

After having lunch at Chez Clément, they travelled to the Notre Dame Cathedral, where they both prayed, although Sally did so with more vigour. Sally prayed that she would perform well in her A-Levels at the end of the academic year and that her relationship with Greg would flourish. Greg prayed that he could make love to Sally. Then, they caught a bus back to the Eiffel Tower, from where they walked to their hotel.

The following day, Greg took Sally for a cruise on the River Seine. They circled Paris for a while before they got off and ate another authentic French meal, which included frog legs. Then they returned to their hotel to pack their suitcases before catching a taxi to the Gare du Nord station. As their taxi weaved through the heavy traffic and alongside the beautiful River Seine, Greg and Sally both had tears in their eyes because they were leaving behind the paradise they had known for the last few days. Still, Greg looked forward to seeing Auntie Ethel. Sally had to admit that she had missed her strict parents.

Within an hour, they were on a train leaving Paris and heading for Calais. Two days later, they were back home in Northwood, eternally grateful for the few days of utter pleasure they had spent in only each other's company.

Ode to Cambridge

Greg quietly slipped into his room on the first floor at Jesus College, Cambridge. Ever since he had arrived at the prestigious university a month earlier, he felt semi-deprived, especially because of the subtle racial discrimination he was subjected to. Not only had the students perpetrated this, but even the tutors.

Aside from that, he was having a wonderful time in this wonderful city surrounded by lush green countryside, pursuing the law degree, which made Auntie Ethel endlessly proud. He found that the fact that he was a law student was a kind of aphrodisiac to the young female students around. He even got some sexual advances from female tutors. Despite all this, he stayed faithful to Sally because he wanted to commit to her for life.

What he looked forward to most were Sally's regular visits, accompanied by their many candlelit dinners. Incredibly, they still had not made love. Sally said that because of her religious beliefs and faith, they should wait until after they got married before they gained carnal knowledge of each other. Greg had increasingly strong sexual urges towards her, and he was hoping that he could change her mind by proposing to her this weekend. Luckily for him, he was a not virgin; he had slept with some of the schoolgirls that he dated whilst he was at Merchant Taylors' School.

He loved both Sally's body and mind. She was reading an economics degree at the London School of Economics. He relished the opportunities he had to take the train to London to visit her every so often.

Sally was due to come up to Cambridge this weekend to visit him. He was really looking forward to taking her punting on the River Cam. Even though it was now autumn, there was many a golden sunset to be had in Cambridge, where one could feel truly at one with nature.

Abruptly there was a ring on the telephone in Greg's room. It was the porter, telling him that there were two young ladies waiting for him at the entrance to the college. Greg was surprised but overjoyed at the prospect of seeing Sally again soon. He wondered who the other lady was. He skipped out of his room and went downstairs to the college entrance. There to his amazement stood Sally holding hands with Greg's former and much younger girlfriend, Joy – an English brunette who attended St Paul's Girls' School in Hammersmith, London. The two had been sworn enemies ever since Sally and Greg had become a couple. So he wondered what was going on.

When all three of them returned to Greg's room, Sally told Greg that she had fallen pregnant. However, she insisted that this happened after she had slept with a French lecturer at LSE. She confessed that she had been two-timing him for the past three months with this older man from Paris, France. He was a French aristocrat, and her family had put a lot of pressure on her to date him with a view to marriage. Greg realised that, despite all Sally's protestations, his race and colour had come into play in dissuading her family from encouraging her to stay true to him.

He was heartbroken and could not keep the tears from streaming down his face. Deep down, he was glad Joy was with them; otherwise he might well have stuck Sally for causing him so much pain – a pain he thought she would never be capable of inflicting.

Later that evening when he told Auntie Ethel of this crisis during their weekly telephone call, she sounded as shocked as he was. "I always thought that Sally was a decent and well-behaved young lady. She must have been led astray by the people she mixed with at university, especially that French lecturer."

"I thought I knew her. She gave me no indication that she was unhappy with our relationship."

Greg's Crisis of
Cultural Identity

The longer Greg lived in England, the more perplexed he became as to whether he should adopt the lifestyle of a white Englishman wholeheartedly or try to include his African heritage in his daily living. Even though he had been born in Kumasi in the Gold Coast, and his parents and relatives had inculcated him with some African culture and mores, naturally he still drew great strength from his links with England. However, as he progressed through his education and legal training, he had less and less contact with black people, and this had a huge impact upon his psyche. He felt more at home with White English people.

Back in the Gold Coast, he had been used to speaking his native Twi often and some Swahili at home with his mother. Despite the fact that he had enjoyed prosperity back in the Gold Coast when his parents were alive, he found his somewhat reduced circumstances in England comfortable. With his impressive qualifications behind him, he had wonderful prospects of living as luxurious and wealthy a lifestyle as he had done when his parents were alive. However, he believed that he could only be happy if he was surrounded by other like-minded White English people.

This cultural development in Greg's lifestyle deeply troubled Auntie Ethel. She realised that Greg had forgotten most of his Swahili and Twi. Furthermore, it irked him when she or his friends reminded him of his past life in the Gold Coast. As far as he was concerned, his initial upbringing in the Gold Coast was not sophisticated enough for the company he wished to keep, and he thought it would impede the progress of his career.

Greg's Gargantuan Efforts to Join the Popular Conservative Party

Greg had been greatly swayed by the influence of the Conservative-leaning family of his best friend from his Merchant Taylor School days, Brian Dunton. As Greg's friendship with Brian deepened, he got more opportunities to spend time with Brian's family. He especially enjoyed his conversations with his father, Sir Peter Dunton.

Sir Peter Dunton's ardent belief in and support of free trade and laissez-faire policies fascinated Greg. Through his studies at Jesus College, Greg had become acquainted with the work of John Maynard Keynes, a onetime Cambridge don, as well as free-market proponents like Adam Smith, and he had become convinced of the merits of their arguments.

Greg's Attempt to Be Selected as a Conservative Candidate for Member of Parliament

One bleak autumn Monday in September 1963, during his train trip to Biggleswade in Bedfordshire, Greg tried to rehearse his campaign speech, which he hoped would persuade the Conservative Association in Biggleswade to choose him as their parliamentary candidate. Greg knew that he was up against four other capable aspirants. However, he doubted if any of them would have his communication skills, which he had honed over several years of legal study and at the bar. He read through his notes on current affairs, especially those concerning Biggleswade and the town council's plans to develop the local area.

Brian had warned him not to be overconfident. He cited his own experience of his surprising failure to be selected as the Conservative candidate for his hometown of Newcastle, despite his family's well-publicised history of providing local MPs.

When Greg arrived at Biggleswade Train station, he asked the railway assistant for directions to the Conservative Association on St Andrews Street. He was greeted with a startled look, after which the man regained his composure and gave him the requisite information. Greg decided to walk the short distance to his destination, to preserve his calm and help him enjoy the emerging autumnal sunshine.

As he arrived at the Conservative Association building, he saw the back of a rotund white woman with flowing strawberry-blond hair. She was also walking towards the entrance of the Conservative Association building. What a beauty! As she was about to open the front door of the building, she turned around. The sight of her took his breath away. He could not believe that he had just seen Sally for the first time in twenty years.

When he entered the lobby of the building five minutes later, he found out that the other candidates had cried off and that she was the only candidate standing against him to be selected as the Conservative parliamentary candidate for the safe seat of North East Bedfordshire. Much to his chagrin, she did not recognise him. He decided not to introduce himself, but within five minutes of conversing with him in the back room to the election podium, she realised who he was. They were both overcome with emotion. Even though they were both passionate about embarking on a political career and having a successful one at that, neither of them wanted to hurt the other's political chances. Who would use their killer instinct and draw first blood?

Thoughts flooded Greg's mind about how long he had waited for an opportunity of a realistic prospect of being elected a Conservative MP. Now he was being presented with such an opportunity, and there was no way he would give it up without a damn good fight.

Stranger than Fiction

Life seemed very bleak for George Ansah. He was the only child of Jason and Emily Ansah. He lived with them in Bedford, his birthplace. His father worked as an accountant at the local firm of George Hay Accountants.

George had spent the last seven years studying hard to become a lawyer. He had always been a clever and diligent student at school, as shown by his success in gaining a scholarship to Bedford Public School and his subsequent prizes there, his GCSE results, and his AS-Level and A-Level results. After his secondary education in Bedfordshire, he had gone on to Bristol University, where he studied law.

He received reasonable marks in his law exams, even though it was a new subject to him, and none of his immediate family had ever studied law or worked in a legal practice. None of his immediate family could help him to understand the new and complex legal concepts he was learning at university as well as the legal terminology. After receiving his LL.B. degree, George went on to the College of Law at Store Street in London, where he studied the legal practise course, which he passed with distinction.

Despite the fact that his distant uncle, Barry Ansah, owned a law firm in West London, he still could not secure a paid legal job anywhere in the UK. Because of the economic recession, Barry's firm was facing ever-dwindling business so that he could only offer his nephew unpaid work experience. George took him up on this offer for a few months, but he knew that he had to take drastic measures if he was to keep his dream of becoming a fully fledged lawyer alive. Even though George had been born in the UK and had also received his education and training at Bristol University, one of the leading law schools in the country of his birth, he had struggled to make headway in finding himself employment in law in the UK. He suffered from occasional bouts of depression because of the incessant discrimination he faced as a result of the profession he wanted to pursue, which did not help.

Barry persuaded George to travel to Ghana, in West Africa, the country of his parents' origin, to see if his legal employment prospects might improve there. Barry said that he knew some lawyers there, who had established some legal chambers, and he thought that they would appreciate someone with George's Western legal training.

George had never travelled to Ghana or, for that matter, to anywhere on the African continent. It was with some trepidation that he decided to embark on his trip to Accra, Ghana, in search of employment. He asked Barry lots of questions about the living conditions there. He also wondered what it would be like working as a lawyer in Ghana. Would he have to wear a wig despite the tropical heat?

With some financial assistance from Uncle Barry, George bought a one-way ticket to Accra from British Airways. George had never even been on a plane before. He wondered what it would be like. The furthest he had travelled was Paris in France; the mode of transport he had used to get there was the Eurostar train. He had been frightened by the battery of vaccinations that he had to have before he could travel to Ghana. He also had to take countless bitter malaria tablets.

When he arrived in Ghana in January 2012, which was in the middle of winter in Europe, he was really glad that he had followed Uncle Barry's advice to come to Ghana to try to find work. He loved the friendly and jovial mannerisms of the Ghanaian natives he met in Accra as well as the legal work that Uncle Barry's lawyer friends were able to give him. Whenever George met or spoke to any native Ghanaians who realised that he was from the UK, they said *"Akwaaba"* to him – meaning "Welcome to Ghana" – and they asked him if it was as easy to make money in the UK as they had heard.

George grew interested in Ghanaian politics. He supported the New Patriotic Party (NPP) but was impressed with the sophistication of the discourse and analysis of politics in Ghanaian media and the fact that presidential and vice-presidential debates including the mainstream political parties – the National Democratic Congress (NDC) and the New Patriotic Party (NPP) flourished in Ghana without let or hindrance.

This was in stark contrast to any other African country. George respected many of the leading politicians, such as the former president John Agyekum Kufuor; the late former president, Professor John Evans Atta-Mills; and the Honourable Nana Akufo-Addo, because they were first and foremost lawyers, who had used their legal knowledge to forge effective and successful political careers, especially using their superior communication skills.

Uncle Barry's lawyer friend in Accra, Mr William Mensah, had advised George Ansah to do a conversion course at the Ghanaian Bar School, which would give him the legal authority to practise as a lawyer in Ghana. The conversion course would last six months. Mr William Mensah offered to pay his fees for the course because he was impressed with George's legal knowledge and analytical mind from their interview shortly after George's arrival in Ghana.

George was looking forward to this conversion course because he thought it would provide him with an excellent opportunity to show that he was much cleverer than all the other law candidates at the Ghanaian Bar School. George also believed that it would help him to come into contact with other similarly well-educated people, who could become good friends of his.

The Tribulations of the Ghanaian Bar Exams

When George joined the other candidates for the Ghanaian bar exams in attending the classes near Makola Market in Accra to prepare for the exams, most of his colleagues treated him as if he was a true *obroni*, much to his disdain. He wanted to be treated as one of his fellow Ghanaians, except that he felt he would have better legal knowledge than they did.

Surprisingly, one month after starting the conversion course, his best friend was a Nigerian woman called Angela, who had moved with her family to live in Ghana when she was three years old. Angela was the eldest of three children of her Nigerian parents, Mr Adebola Yusuf and Mrs Yinka Yusuf, who both originated from the Lagos area in Nigeria. They were both Yoruba and born-again Christians, and they encouraged their children, including Angela, to follow their parents' faith.

Angela had two younger brothers, both obsessed with being businessmen like their father. Although Angela had undergone her secondary education in Ghana at Achimota School, she went back to Nigeria, to the University of Lagos, to study law there, using the very good West African A-Level results she had received (A,A,A). After completing her LL.B. degree at the University of Lagos, she had trained as a lawyer at the Nigerian legal bar. After this, she decided that she wanted to qualify as a lawyer in Ghana as well because most of her immediate family lived there.

Having been brought up with the dual heritage and culture of Ghana and Nigeria, Angela seemed to appreciate George's internationalism. Even though he had made a few more friends, like Kwaku, who hailed from Sunyani in Brong Ahafo, with whom he regularly played football on a dusty nearby football pitch, the person with whom George soon felt a real rapport was Angela. After another month of the conversion course, George's friendship with Angela turned into a beautiful romance. It reached a point where they could hardly bear to be without each other's company. In spite of their hard work at the Ghanaian conversion course and at reviewing the Ghanaian legal materials, especially the 1992 Ghanaian constitution, they always seemed to find time to go out on dates at fashionable places, such as Frankie's and Next Door, as well as relaxing by the sea at Labadi Beach.

The end of the Ghanaian bar conversion course was soon upon George. On the day of the first exam, he panicked because he had not reviewed for these exams as much as he would normally prepare for an exam. Angela was much more confident and reassured him that he would be fine. She gave him a big kiss and a warm hug before they entered the exam room. One and a half weeks later, these law exams were behind them.

George returned to working for Mr William Mensah whilst he waited for his conversion law exam results. Angela had been offered a temporary lecturer's job at the University of Ghana. She had grabbed this opportunity to impart some of her legal knowledge and to do research so that she could publish some legal articles. However, within a month or so, both George and Angela were increasingly drawn to the activities of the New Patriotic Party (NPP), and they began to attend political rallies together.

Marital Bliss?

A few weeks later, George asked Angela's parents, Adebola and Yinka Yusuf, for their daughter's hand in marriage. They were glad that she had met such an intelligent and dynamic young man, and they readily gave their blessings. By October 2012, they had been married at the Chapel at Ridge Church School in Accra. They waited until after they were married before they moved in together.

George's parents had travelled from Bedfordshire in the UK to attend their only child's wedding. His mother sobbed with joy throughout the wedding ceremony. Angela's father, Adebola, being a wealthy Nigerian businessman dealing in the export and import of oil, cocoa, and diamonds, bought George and Angela a three-bedroom house in the Regimanuel estate as a wedding gift. George and Angela willingly accepted this gift, amongst many others from friends and family.

After George and Angela's continued association with the NPP, they were told that a new NPP candidate for the Adenta constituency was needed for the forthcoming parliamentary elections in December 2012. George and Angela had numerous arguments over a whole week behind closed doors about which of them should seek the NPP candidacy. George wished that through their frequent lovemaking, Angela would become pregnant, thereby scuppering her immediate political ambitions. However, unbeknownst to him, Angela had been using contraception – the pill – because she wanted to develop her career before giving birth to children. Eventually, they decided on the flip of a coin that Angela would seek the NPP candidacy in the Adenta constituency this time, and George would try to get elected as an MP in the near future.

In the parliamentary elections of December 2012, Angela Ansah won the parliamentary seat in Adenta so that her political career took off. George started to focus more on playing a low-key role in NPP meetings and on furthering his legal career so as not to distract attention from his wife. He wondered when he and Angela would ever have children. How could a coin toss have been so cruel in denying him the political career he longed for so desperately!

About the Author

Mr Kwabena Date-Bah is a British lawyer, originally from Ghana in West Africa. He was educated at Berkhamsted Public School; University College, London; Keele University; and Cass Business School in City University in London. He has worked in real estate for a number of years.